Rook

The Broken Bows, Volume 1

Kerri Ann

Published by Kerri Ann, 2018.

This is a work of fiction. Similarities to real people, places, or events are entirely coincidental.

ROOK

First edition. July 8, 2018.

Copyright © 2018 Kerri Ann.

ISBN: 979-8227527257

Written by Kerri Ann.

Also by Kerri Ann

The Broken Bows
Rook
King

Watch for more at https://www.authorkerriann.com.

Chapter One

"FORGIVE ME, FATHER, for I have sinned," the small voice from the other side of the screen confided. I can just make out her shadow as she completes the sign of the cross. "Today marks the fifteenth day since my last confession. My last mass was three weeks ago, and I have one sin to atone for."

"Tell me your troubles, child." I know it's fruitless to ask, but it's expected. Their whole reason for appearing here is to be absolved.

"I had impure thoughts about a woman in my...book club," she says cautiously.

"Are you lying, child?"

"Father, I'm telling you what I feel comfortable with you knowing." So, she's another one of *them.*

"Continue, child."

She clears her throat. "You see, we were reading a book about first loves. It was about a woman, and how her best friend was the first to really *see* her through all her faults. Her problems didn't matter. Seeing love conquer and repair damages, she came to love the other woman—in the story, that is. Love can be pure in so many ways. Right, Father?"

"Yes, child. I agree that love can be pure of heart, but not sexual in its context, such as love thy brother, love thy sister. What is it, though, that has made you feel impure? Tell me. Tell your God what it is so that you may repent." Every day, all day, this is the possible outcome of so many lives in our city. These lost souls need our care, and it's my job to make them whole. They need to feel loved and cherished without reservation or condemnation.

"Well, Father, I've never felt that from a man. It made me feel secure and cared for by this woman. She makes me feel like I'm perfect. I *know* in my heart that God would tell me if this love is wrong. But if love is good in all forms, then why deny me a love if he presents it?"

And there's the predicament of my position. How can I deny love? How do I tell her that it's an abomination to love another woman in the way that she does? I do the will of God because it's right and just. "What you personally feel is different than the scriptures, my dear child. Loving in a chaste way is expected and condoned, but to love her in the way that a man and a woman would is unwell in the eyes of God."

"But Father, what of the changes under the Pope, the holiest of Fathers on earth? Hasn't he stated that all love is to be cherished? Why deny me? My confession isn't in loving *her*, my confession is this; In loving her, the love for my husband has become secondary. I love him, I do, but I can't love him as I love her. Do you understand, Father?"

So, it's not that she loves this woman, it's that she's venturing out of her marriage. Well, this one's cut and dry. "This is an impure allowance under God and his teachings. You must care for your wedding vows. You will work on giving your husband the love and devotion that you imparted when you first married him. You gave your word that his love was the only love, other than that of your God."

"Yes, Father." Her voice falls. Seeing her bowing her head in defeat, I wonder...did she really feel that her confession would be seen as a just reason to venture from wedlock and step out of the marriage? These are the situations I deal with, and it pains me. Our parish is in a more volatile area of the city, which brings these creatures of faithlessness to our door often.

"You will repent your sins through your act of contrition. Repeat after me, 'Heavenly Father, I in good faith will follow the path of your teachings, and in doing so, I will work on being a good person that puts effort into my marriage.'" She quietly repeats what I say, and I continue. "I will no longer have impure thoughts about another, as it is unfair to my vows under God." She again repeats after me, and in doing so, I hear her voice becoming stronger; more willful.

"You will perform six hail Mary's and continue to work on your family obligation. I absolve you of your sins. In the name of the Father, and of the Son, and of the Holy Spirit. Amen."

"Amen. Thank you, Father." Rising out of the booth, she closes the door behind her while I relax with another completed parishioner on the right path. Do I analyze every one of these sad souls? Yes. I care for them, not only as their direct link to Christ, but I also feel their pain and sorrow as their priest.

There are days that these burdens weigh heavily on my soul, and that I despair with the inflicted damage on my own psyche. My lord keeps me strong, or as strong as he can. And what I cannot handle, I contain in my own way.

Her love of the woman could be a product of a bad relationship. The dangerous liaison could be nothing more than her looking for love where love hasn't been found yet. Nervously rubbing the sleeve of my robes, I take a deep breath and blow it out. I'll deal with the dark thoughts I have about her and the love she has later when I'm alone.

As the door next to me opens and closes again, a man enters. "Forgive me, Father, for I have sinned."

Garnering my composure to assist another lost soul once more, I situate myself in the confessional to take on their needs. "Tell me how I can help you, son."

"It's been six months since my last confession." His voice is deep and gruff. His voice has a dangerous tone that's truly recognizable—hardened and callous.

Answering him in a calm manner, I say, "Six months is a long time. How many confessions will we address today?"

The screen doesn't allow room for me to see his face, but I can see his profile. I know who he is. Bracken Madox, President of the Broken Bows MC. His club runs the south side of the city with an iron will, and even heavier fist. They deal in guns, drugs, and sex trading. He's a dangerous man.

"Only those I wish you to know, Father." Bracken and I have history, and I both love and loathe when he visits.

"To absolve you, I would expect nothing more than full honesty, my son."

He laughs darkly. "How about I give you what I can, Father. The rest is for you to read between the lines. I think my wife is stepping out. Mostly my fault. I think I push her to it."

Great. The woman that was here is his wife. Just the darkness I needed today. Thank you, Father, for giving me a further trial of piety.

"Knowing if she has stepped out is not yours to confess. Tell me your confession, son."

"You're right, Father." His sinister voice booms off the walls of our tiny enclosure. "My sins are extensive. How long do you have?"

I don't doubt they are. Lifting the edge of my cassock, I scratch the scars on my wrist. "As long as you need, son."

"Well, let's get started then, shall we?" Laying his long legs out in front of him, Bracken crosses his ankles, settling in for a long conversation. "My first sin, of course, has multiple infractions. Sins of the flesh. I love flesh. I've partaken in free pussy that would make your robes curl, Father. The taste of that sweet nectar as it glides along your tongue? Mmm, exquisite. The feel of supple tits as they're pinched, fucked, scarred and sucked? The heavy screams as they ask to be released? Yeah, that's both dangerous and intoxicating. But you wouldn't understand that, would you, *Kyden*? No. You wouldn't know the feel of a woman's cunt anymore. You walked away from that."

Walking isn't the right, I ran. Slipping away in the middle of the night, I left, never looking back. He knows that every time he explains his sins, the effect is meant to shock. He understands it more than any other could. He knows me. A woman's touch is not what I need, though I'd love it. The reminder is fresh every moment. Clearing my throat, I try to bring the conversation back to something more suitable for the venue. "Thank you for the honesty, son. You stated multiple sins—"

"Yes, that I did. I've been having difficulties expressing my rage. It comes out in fits of destructiveness." His tone is excited. I can almost see his snarky grin.

"You have released this rage on others, I assume?" Catching my nail on one of the more recent scars, I revel at the pain it elicits.

"Goddamn right I have."

"We do not take the Father's name in vain here, son. Please refrain from blaspheme, or I'll have to ask you to leave without completing your penance."

"Yes, Priest. I understand the consequences." Uncrossing his ankles and shifting forward on the seat, Bracken brings his face close to the screen. "I understand perfectly."

"Good. Continue, please."

"Well, Father, I've unfortunately harmed a few poor souls in my care."

"Harming others is not permitted. Do unto others as you wish done upon you. Follow the path of God's will and you will find absolution."

"I think I'm past the point of absolution. Don't you, Ky?"

"My name is Father Kyden. Please, use it correctly, son."

"Yes, Father Kyden. Thank you for the reminder." His voluminous voice surrounds me, pulling me down that dangerous edge. The reason I became a priest was because of men like him. My darkness envelopes me the same way as his harnesses the truly dangerous parts of him by feeding him, fueling his need for mayhem. "Well, you see, there have been casualties left in my wake. A multitude of corpses. Some I killed with my bare hands, others I had decommissioned by the hands of another, but I was the instrument. Can I be absolved of those sins, Father?"

The itch on my skin is a burning need, a harsh fire of release cresting under the surface. Forcing my hands away and laying them in my lap, I do my best to avoid the need to drive out my inner demons.

Knowing Bracken doesn't wish to repent is not a part of the confessional, though I do wish it were. There's no savior that could clear the taint on Bracken's soul. The devil has held him tight to his bosom for far too long. "I will pray for you, son. Beyond that, it is up to you to repent and see to your own eternal soul. God cannot help you if you do not attempt to atone."

"Understood. Thank you." The glee is palpable in his voice. He's enjoying this far too much.

"Is that the extent of your sins?"

Shaking his head, he looks directly at me. "No, Father. No, no, no, no. I have partaken in one of the worst sins that one can. I've tainted one of God's children that felt they were unattainable." Scratching his fingers down the screen, popping over the holes one by one, slowly, he peers through and glares at me. "I've tainted the soul of a priest. I've reminded him of what he's hiding from, what it is that he covets. What he wishes for. What his *darkest* desires are." The darkness of evil is visible in his gaze as he stares through the screen. I feel the inky darkness he talks of, the unwanted caresses that make me shake.

"Who is it that you've tainted, son?"

Sitting back hard against the confessional cabinet, it vibrates under his weight. "You, brother. It may not be today, but it will be soon. You've hidden for long enough. Come home." Rising quickly to his feet, he exits the confessional before I can respond.

Chapter Two

AFTER BRACKEN LEFT, I had three other parishioners for soft-minded confessional, two families request baptisms, and a confirmation lined up for the Sunday coming. It was a long day. I was exhausted, to be honest, as Bracken takes a lot out of a soul.

Getting to my quarters was not only a welcome reprieve, it was a necessary component of my evening. Removing my tippet and hanging it on the hook inside the door, I undo the thirty-three buttons on my cassock one by one. Counting them down gives me a sense of peace, and the release helps me deal with the demons I fight every day. Moving it to the hanger, I gently lay it across, giving it the respect it deserves. It reminds me of what I am—*who* I am. I'm no longer controlled by the wills of those that sin, that I have become a better person through reflection and atonement of my stray mind.

Changing into more comfortable attire, I set the kettle on the stove and toast a few slices of bread before grabbing a glass of holy wine to unwind. This is my daily routine. They're necessary to survive. No one will ever know of my demons. *No one.* There's a ritualistic component to my process, but it keeps me on the path of righteousness in the eyes of God. Or, at least, that's how I feel. It helps me to cope and to assist those in my care for another day.

Grabbing the hot bread as it rises, I butter it lightly before placing it on a plate. Walking to my living room, I lay out my meager meal and kneel down in front of the cross that adorns my mantle. The fire has long since died down in the hearth and that's just fine on this warm spring evening. The less light visible in the room, the better for me.

"In the name of the Father, and of the Son, and of the Holy Spirit. Amen. Forgive me Father for I have sinned. Please accept my confession for the impure thoughts that I have partaken in this day." I pick up the neatly wrapped, rolled, and tied leather case. "My perspective on the world was tried again today, Father. Why do you try my resolve daily?"

I know the answer, though I don't wish to believe it. Christ understands my failures and accepts them; therefore, my penance must be justified. Laying out the towel I use—that no one knows of—I prepare. Unwrapping the tie and laying out the kit, I roll up my right sleeve. "Today was especially difficult, Father. I understood her driving need for love. I felt that in her heart she was truly satisfied in the arms of another. I felt challenged by the trials you set forth today. Thank you."

Selecting my favorite tool, I place it across my marked and scarred skin, dragging it down the length to exorcise the demon that resides. Watching the darkness escape slowly in light streams down my skin, I feel the excitement and erotic release of the demon fighting to stay. He fights daily to live within me, yet this removes him, for however a short time it is.

Undoing the clasp on my trousers, I reach inside and grab my heated cock as I watch the blood hit the towel below. At first, this didn't occur, but over time, the releasing demon, and God, requested more of me. More pain. Stroking it lightly at first, then harder, I cut myself once more. The pain is not diminishing the envious need for sexual release with a woman. To have a woman, or a multitude of women, did nothing to cool my blood. Stroking harder and harder, I push down until the circumcised head feels like its ripping apart. The sweetness of it is both exhilarating and excruciating. "Give me the tools to release the demon that makes me wish for more, Father. Please," I beg.

Pushing my trousers lower, I cut the inside of my leg, taking the pain deeper. "Forgive me Father for my sins!" I holler. Thankfully, this is helping tonight.

I cannot stomach food or drink without completing my penance. I've tried, but food fails me, expelling immediately. Pumping my hand hotly, again I cut my leg, bringing my orgasm to the forefront. "Thank you. I understand my penance for wishing for more than you have offered. Thank you."

As the ending nears, I rise to my knees and pump the evil seed into the soot. Watching the diaphanous liquid blend with the burned remains, I feel relief. Wiping up with the towel, then sopping up the blood that mars my dark skin, I accept the respite on my tortured soul. Doing up my trousers, pulling down the sleeve of my shirt, I contain the tools until I require them further.

Rolling it up and placing it in position for tomorrow's need, I take a seat in my chair. "Father of all, God on high, please bless this food and drink that I'm about to eat. Thank you for your penance. Thank you for the blessing of helping others and assisting them in becoming better Christians. The trials you set forth for me are many and great. Thank you for that, Lord, and I appreciate all that you do." I cross myself. "In the name of the Father, and of the Son, and of the Holy Spirit. In Christ's name, O' Lord. Amen."

Chapter Three

TODAY, AGAIN, HAS BEEN a blessing in disguise. The morning started off blissfully well. The youngsters that attend the daycare with the good Sisters were fantastic. Each of them performed the sacraments without giggling or silliness. They attended the early mass admirably, and left without a single word spoken of chastisement.

We don't have a large congregation in this area of town, as there are few that feel their eternal souls require pious attention. We're located between whorehouses, strip clubs, cocaine shops, low income tenements, and the Broken Bows MC. Most don't give us the time of day, other than to tag the walls of the rectory with graffiti. I've had to clear it this week alone three times, and it's only Tuesday.

Most days, I don't go to the confessional until the afternoon, as a great deal of our inhabitants don't wake until after eleven. There's no use in being there early.

This morning, my fresh scabs are itchy, pulling at the skin, tearing at my resolve to run back to my residence to skim the blade over flesh once more. But I have will of the mind and soul. I can wait.

Walking through the pews, acknowledging those that stop by for a quick prayer or blessing, I'm anticipating the joyousness that helping all of God's children gives me.

"Father. Could I confess?"

Turning around, I take in the dark-haired beauty with creamy brown eyes. I'd know those eyes anywhere. She stands, waiting for my response.

With a weak smile, I feel my heart fall deep. "Of course you can."

Motioning her forward, I watch her ass sway as she takes steps within the pew rows toward the confessional booth. My breathing is tight, my soul crushes, and my heart is racing at a beat I can't time.

Wandering into the booth, she closes herself in as I gather my resolve before walking to my side.

Sitting down, the window is closed. As Scarlet opens it, the light streams in. It's been some time since I've seen Scarlet this close, the brilliant light from the church sends light dancing across her legs.

"Forgive me, Father, for I have sinned." Her sultry voice bounces around my head and off the wooden cage that holds me in.

"How may I help you, child."

"Father, I have impure thoughts about a man I cannot have." I know she's not married. Scarlet doesn't have a man in her life, that I know for certain.

"Tell me of your sin, child. Let me help you."

Letting out a haughty breath, Scarlet shifts slightly on her seat. "I had a dream the other night. The dream was so real that I woke up wet and aroused."

Licking my lips, I lean forward on the seat to get a better listen. "Continue. Let me see if I can help."

"Well, you see, I'm not sure I can tell you all of it, Father. It's very in-depth."

Father, give me strength. Of course it is. "Please." My mind is clouded over, thinking of nothing more than that one word.

"So, in the dream, the man's face is obscured. I know who it is, but the suspense of it makes the dream more intense. Lying there, spread out on the bed, he licked my most intimate parts as if he were a starved man. He told me that without it, he would perish, so I allowed him to continue. The heat kissed every nerve in my body as it tingled. My toes curled, my legs felt like rubber, and my heart beat to a tempo I'd never felt."

Sitting forward has become excruciating as I lean my balls against the back of the confessional chair. My cock strains against the cloth of my trousers, causing a tenting effect that I have no way of appeasing in this confined space.

"Tell me more, child." Saying "child" seems incorrect in this venue, but I continue with the pretense. I know it's Scarlet, and that it's the proper conversation as parishioner and priest.

"Well, you see, he never spoke. But he directed me to his will with a force that I thought unattainable. Caressing my body, masterfully touching me in places that brought every sound I could muster out of me…I was enjoying it, though I knew it was wrong. I know that the act of intercourse with a man out of wedlock is forbidden and frowned upon."

Jesus in heaven, this woman tempts me. I'm not sure I can halt my hand from gaining purchase of my cock as she speaks. Pushing it low, the mere action causes me severe strain. Looking over, Scarlet's hands are roaming across her ample chest, along her legs, and lifting her tight red dress high enough to see the edge of her haltered pantyhose. I shouldn't look.

Why does the devil tempt me so?

"Continue, Scarlet." My voice is low and strained as I contain my composure in this very heated situation. Any other woman, I'd not want the details of her rapture, but Scarlet, she is my Eve. Temptation and blaspheme all tied up in what I can never have—*should* never have.

Pushing the edge of her tight dress higher, I see that she isn't wearing any panties, showcasing her neatly trimmed sex. Glistening, her hands search between the folds as I watch like a dirty voyeur. How do I stop this? Can I stop this? The temptation is almost too much.

She pants heavily. "Well, kissing me here gave me a rush like no other. I don't know if the feeling is wrong, or if it's a blessing from God that I was able to enjoy something so great alone. I was tempted." Stroking herself, she pauses. "So tempted to call the man in question to alert him to the dream that rocked me so spiritually."

Rocking her finger back and forth, I unintentionally grip my cock in hand. Pulling it between my clothing, I feel the danger of what is happening here. It excites me more than the cutting has ever done. Unable to tear my eyes from her ministrations, I quickly undo the button on my pants. Reaching in, I grasp it as if it's the asp in the story of Adam and Eve, torturing it with angry strokes.

"Kyden, the man was you. It's always been you, never anyone else in my dreams. Touching me, stroking me, wetting my appetite for more." Stroking harder and harder, our movements become fast as she brings herself to the edge of ecstasy. "Father, forgive me, for I have sinned!" she yells out as I spill my seed across the floor of the confessional.

Fuck. I've never felt such passion and release in the act of making myself come. Watching her come undone was erotic in more ways that I can ever name. Tonight, I'll have to complete further penance than normal to override this tremendous sin.

Straightening her outfit, I watch Scarlet become serene and poised once more. The pious beauty that I see sitting in the front pews weekly, taking the sacraments into her hot mouth, makes me wish it were my cock.

Tucking my flaccid penis back into my pants, I do my best to calm my overheated blood. I can't let the parishioners see me like this when I exit.

"My child, I understand your dangerous position. A dream is only a dream. You cannot be held responsible for a machination of the mind. The devil works in mysterious ways, and I feel this was his way of gaining purchase into your mind, feeding you with a seed of deceit. Do not put too much thought into it. As penance, through your act of contrition, repeat after me, 'My Holy Father, I in good faith will follow the path of your teachings, saying three hail Mary's.' You will try to get more sleep. The devil cannot enter your dreams when you are well-rested."

Saying as directed, Scarlet adds before leaving, "Thank you, Father. I will do as you've said."

As she rises from the chair and exits the confessional, I slump against the wall, releasing the pent-up breath I've been holding. Of all the women in all the gin joints, she had to walk into mine. Now I know why he stated such a line.

The things I envy others for.

Chapter Four

THE REMAINDER OF MY week has been uneventful. Scarlet didn't return, and Bracken was away, giving me nothing further to ponder about. And the good Sisters had prepared a large dinner for our youth group meeting that went off without a hitch.

Now that it's Sunday, I'm truly looking forward to the act of following in the scriptures. The night after seeing Scarlet, I pushed on my cock so hard I tore it. The pain of my penance was justified. For allowing myself the satisfaction of the skin with another, I had betrayed my vow. I've never taken the vow of celibacy, but I'd always promised that love would be unattainable for one such as me. I was offended that I'd allowed such a movement, and had therefore allowed the devil purchase within my soul further. My right arm and legs have taken a beating with the punishments necessary to get over the dangers of the flesh. By Friday, feeling refreshed, appeased that my conscience was clean, I fell into the position of helping others with a fervor.

The parish has been filling up quickly this morning. The average Sunday finds us half-filled on one side, and maybe only two or three rows on the other. This week is different. It gives me joy to know that my personal atonement may be part of the reason for such an act of attendance. I could be wrong, but it feels good to know they're filling the pews for whatever reason.

Standing at the front, greeting each parishioner as they enter, gives me a moment to connect with them before the mass. Yes, I will say goodbye to them as well, but this gives me a better gauge of those that require the confessional. So far, I've singled out three that couldn't even look me in the eyes, so I'll watch them throughout the full reading and sacraments.

"Hello, Father. We're very glad to join you today."

I grin, glad that they've attended. "Welcome, Bracken." Shaking his hand as I take in his malicious smile, I turn to the woman beside him.

Her sallow cheeks and dark eyes, with thick makeup covering her bruises show the abuse she's recently taken. Being on the receiving end of someone such as Bracken can't be easy. "And who is this lovely woman on your arm?"

Turning to her, Bracken replies, "This is my wife, Christy. Say hello to the good Father."

Keeping her gaze trained on the ground, she slowly raises her eyes to me. "It's nice to meet you, Father. I've heard many lovely things about you."

"I'm sorry that we've never had a chance to meet before. How long have you been married?" Looking to Bracken for approval, she smiles, but it's weak.

"Just over a month, Father."

"Newly wedded it seems." Giving her a slight smile, I look to Bracken. His evil glare hasn't left hers the whole time we've stood here talking. He watches her like hawk watches its meal.

"We are. Very happily, too." Smiling up at Bracken, I can see the strain in her demeanor. Showcasing rotted teeth, I know the woman has had a hard life, which hasn't been made any easier by marrying the likes of him.

He nods his approval at her answer. "Good girl. How about you take a seat beside Fletch. I'll be over after I have a conversation with Father Kyden."

Accepting her dismissal, walking off relieved, Christy wanders to the holy water font before sitting in the pew as directed.

He speaks to me in a low tone. "We need to have a conversation later today, brother." Tucking in close, as if he's about to give me a hug, he says, "Don't avoid me. It's been a week and I've been patient." Stepping back, the same sinister glower as before is there. The devil works its way into those that allow him entrance, and Bracken is a tool of his. With a wink, Bracken moves into my space. "I know she visited you. She *won't* be absolved again, Father. Her next infraction will be her last." Taking in his face, I see the man I once knew almost as well as myself. Dark scars run the length of his jaw, travelling the length of the right side of his face, reminding me of life in that society. The reinforcement of their rules are absolute.

Smiling as sweetly as possible—as there are more eyes than his watching—I appreciate the connotation of harm that he speaks of. "Thank you, son. I will keep that in mind for future endeavors. Blessed be those who follow the path of righteousness."

"Blessed is the arrow that strikes true." Speaking his club motto, he steps away, leaving me with a need to atone again, now more than ever.

Greeting more of the congregation as they enter the hallowed halls, I push his warnings to the back of my mind. Allowing the last of them to say their good mornings to me, I finally traverse to the front for the Mass.

Chapter Five

AFTER THANKING THE Lord for his guidance in today's Mass, and after all the refreshed and repented parishioners have left, I still have *so* much more to do. Namely, swimming through all the lost souls waiting their turn for the confessional.

Feeling the weight of this past week, and seeing Scarlet sitting in the front like she always does, but in a new light, I feel my soul is tainted. I've seen more of her than I should. Only her God or husband-to-be should see what I now have. Yes, I'm the divining rod to the Lord in this house of worship, but it was not something of mine. It was a *just* trial. I passed through the test, only barely.

As the first person enters the confessional, I walk over. He's not a member of our usual congregation, but I did notice him at the beginning of the day. The rest of the penitents are giving privacy by staying in areas closer to the front, away from where the absolutions are considered. Touching the edge of a scar, just by my wrist, I say a silent prayer to give me strength of will through all of it.

Acknowledging them as I pass by, I tuck the front of my cassock low to hide my marks. These are my penance, and no one but God's to know of.

Stepping in, I settle on the bench and slide the window screen back. "Hello, my child."

"Hello, Father. Forgive me for my sins. This week has been especially difficult, and I'm afraid my penance will be great," the man on the other side of the screen states.

"Tell me, son, and I will let God be the judge of your absolution."

"Well, Father, I...I coveted another woman."

"In what way did this occur?"

"You see, Father, my wife and I have been married for five glorious years, and in that time, we've tried everything in our power to become parents. Not one of the trials, tests, or products have been able to assist in our attempt to nurture a child of our own."

"Have you thought of adoption?"

"We have, Father, but it's something that we felt was our last resort. Why would God not grant it to us? We have always been devout children in the house of God."

"Perhaps it is God's will that you assist a child to be with a family that was not intended originally for them. Show them the love you would for any child." Pausing, I hear him sobbing softly. "This sin you speak of, it has been a heavy burden to bear, has it not? Tell me of the sin."

I'd always felt that Scarlet would make a fantastic mother. She's kind, soulful, devout to our God, and would be understanding of the needs I have. But I've never considered it mine to own. God's will has kept me on this path.

The discomfort in my cock increases as I think of Scarlet in a way that is not mine. As the scabs pull at the skin, reminding me that she's not something for me to covet, I continue with the penitent. "Continue, son. I can't ask for your forgiveness and allow your absolution without knowing the sin you speak of."

"There's a woman in our bible study group that has plagued my dreams. Her milky soft skin, her caramel eyes, beautiful hair that is perfection. She makes me want her. I've had impure dreams that continued on to my waking hours. My thoughts and dreams are plagued, Father. I haven't touched my wife in weeks. Help me, please. Help me find serenity."

His mind is fouled and his soul is as tainted as mine. This will require a sacrifice of the soul to expunge the devil. Do I feel for him? Yes. Do I wish that a family of my own were in the cards? Yes. I wish to undo the past and to correct my previous flaws.

Scratching open the scars, feeling the skin burn, I remind myself that it is a sin to covet that which is unattainable. "You need to attend your wife. Take her to dinner, make her dinner, or simply invite her to coffee.

Talk. Find a common ground where you can speak of the ideas that plague your heart. Repel the devil that is staining your marriage."

"Yes, Father."

"Yes, a family is important, but you did not in your vows of marriage promise to give her children, nor did she promise that to you. It was a promise to love in sickness and in health. This is a sickness that you need to overcome. Repeat after me, son, 'I will work on my marriage, giving my wife the due she is deserving of.' Say three Hail Mary's for three days, and work on loving your wife. As well, I would suggest you *find* a way to avoid the bible group for a while. Just until you can feel secure in the denial of her flesh."

Wiping away the tears from his face, he repeats the line I requested before saying, "Thank you, Father, for your guidance and support. God has selected a correct guide to help his lost and wandering souls." Rising from the booth, he leaves. I feel satisfied in the outcome for the man. Hopefully, when he returns to us next week, he will feel better in his marriage and his relationship with God. He's been selected for trials that are difficult for many.

As a new parishioner steps in, I see it is a woman. "Forgive me, Father, for I have sinned. This week marks the fifth week since my last confession and I'm in need of your guidance."

"Tell me, my child."

As she goes through the list of her extensive sins, I catalogue and give directions for her penance according to each sin. They're as most of our locals, that of debauchery, willful harm of another, theft, and jealousy. After she has left, I too feel jealous for the lives they lead. Each are wandering through life with disregard for those they harm. They pause by their rectory, as if we're a Starbucks drive-thru for their sins to be cleared away, only to begin anew. We're the entrance to hell now. All the dangerous and foul creatures that enter my confessional I feel for, but at the same time, I believe that truly none feel penitent.

As the last is cared for, I return to my residence to accept and absolve myself of the sins that have plagued my own soul today. Setting it all out as neatly as the last day, I prepare my meal, my station in front of the dying fire, and ask God for forgiveness. "Today was difficult, Father. Why do you torture me with souls that I cannot look to save? They are not redeemable. Their souls are tainted from years of fake absolutions and it tires me. Please, free me from this." Cutting a deep line along my forearm, I feel the rush of the blade as it peels raw skin. Dripping to the deeply stained, yet cleansed towel, my soul feels no lighter.

"Has it not been enough?" After the raw beating that I gave my member the past Tuesday, I have yet to touch it in a releasing way. I've felt the acceptance from the blood leeching out, and that nothing more was required. Why tonight does he feel more is needed? "Perhaps, Father, I had coveted jealousy in my heart. Was wishing for a family of my own wrong?" I feel the rush of my savior accepting my further need for penitence and understand. "Yes, I understand, Father."

Unclasping my pants, feeling the tight skin that is aching to be left alone, I understand my wants are not my own. For true absolution, I must do as requested. Stroking it slowly at first, pushing past the pain, it grows engorged. A deep relief is felt within me, but it's not enough, not yet. That I know. Gathering up one of the serrated blades, pushing my trousers to the floor, I drag the edge along the inseam of my leg. Matching one's previously, the jagged line seeps ichor. Groaning out at the release, tightening my grip, I think of Scarlet. She would be proud of me for finding a way to expel the demons that taint my soul, that make me a darkened soul in the army of the devil.

Pushing and pulling harder and harder, I cut another, then another, before finally releasing into the soot. I growl out, feeling absolved of my past transgressions.

As the final spasms shudder my earthly form, a knock at the door surprises me. No one bothers me in the residence. It's been expressly requested that once I retire, I am to be left alone.

The door creaks open. "Father, we need you."

Scrambling to clear up my ritual evening activity, the person I'd hoped would never enter has.

"Oh. Father? I'm..." Averting her gaze, Scarlet's voice is one of shock and pain before she gathers her composure. "I'm sorry, truly, but we need you immediately in the church."

Wiping down my arm and leg, pulling up my trousers, I rise from the floor, directing my attention fully upon her. "What is so important that you had to interrupt me in residence after hours, Ms. Grady?" Addressing her formally, her demeanor changes drastically.

"Father, if you're finished with your..." Looking over my shoulder at the dinner laid out on a tray, "meal, we could use you for a poor soul that will need the last rites granted."

Garnering my composure, gathering up my cassock and tippet, I follow Scarlet out to prepare a soul to meet its maker.

Chapter Six

WALKING IN, THE CHAPEL is filled with bikers from Bracken's Broken Bows. They range in age from elders, to those that are considered newer recruits. Some are men and women that I've known since childhood, while others are unknown to me—unfaithful, unrepentant members of society. The worst of the worst. Dangerous to anyone that is not of their credence. Faith only resides in the motto of the club; you stand by your brothers at all costs.

Checking to make sure I'm still following her into the chapel, Scarlet stops at the font, crossing herself with the blessing of God. Doing the same, approaching the mass of hardened career offenders, I wait for them to part like the Dead Sea of old. Nodding to a few of them, they tip their heads or growl as I pass. There's no lost love with some. To most, I betrayed the club, venturing far afield.

Looking to the makeshift pallet, the man I'd hoped to never set eyes on again rests near death. Stopping, glaring at a few men in the crowd, I search out Bracken.

Finding him kneeling to the side, holding the hand of the dying man, I ask crassly, "Why? Why bring him here?"

"Do not all God's children deserve a chance at redemption?" Tossing my words back in my face, Bracken's face shows mirth and mischief.

I ignore his quip. "Why send Scarlet?"

"Because I knew you'd tell me to piss off."

"You're damn right I would!" Covering my mouth after swearing in the house of God, I despise myself for the reactions that Bracken pulls from me unbidden.

Softening at the loss of my composure, Bracken stands to his full height. "Be Father Kyden. Don't be DG's son right now."

He's reminding me that the Devil's Guide, or DG as he's known in the club, is the man laid out in front of me, the retired president of the Broken Bows. Quint Madox, my father.

Without a word, turning from the group and venturing to the altar, I bend down on the kneeling bench to pray. "Kyden!" Bracken calls out, but I continue my course.

"Father, Almighty God. Please give me the strength to send this soul to your bosom. In my *heart,* I know he has not been a good catholic son to you. He has been willful, monstrous in his actions toward others, and with pure malice in his heart which has damaged all those in his care. Grant me the power to do as you bid. In Christ's name, O' Lord. Amen." Rising with a renewed fortitude of purpose, brushing down my outfit, I walk back to those waiting. Scarlet stands just at the edge of those gathered, ready to speak an apology.

"It's fine, Scarlet. I know the pressures of this family. You did what you had to. I don't fault you." Smiling weakly at her, I sidestep the remainder of this pallid funeral as they allow me to pass.

Looking down at Quint, I see the damage. He has multiple gunshots wounds to his chest, where blood bubbles out of the holes. With any other member, they'd have taken them to the hospital or had their resident doc come by to patch him up. Quint has been dying of lung cancer, and in no way will this end well.

Pulling the small vial of holy water from my pocket, I start the final rites on my patriarch. "I believe in God the Father Almighty, Maker of Heaven and Earth. And in Jesus, his only begotten Son; our Lord..." Pausing, I take a deep breath. My will leaves me. Why is it that my family can direct me to do their bidding in such a way that I feel obligated when I *know* in my soul it isn't right? I should've left here. I should have left town to work in a new area with new souls to help. But it felt best to help those that I *knew* of their troubles.

Stopping, I stand upright and bend at the waist, speaking loud enough for his lost soul to hear. "I contain the power to send your soul on, but not the heart to send such a damned one as this to the gates of anywhere but hell. You were an asshole in life, and in death I hope that your maker takes pity on you as you reach his gates." Tossing the holy water as I should, I've given him the best rites I can. "In the name of the Father, and of the Son, and of the Holy Spirit. Amen."

Seeing him staring blankly, searching for absolution from me, the satisfaction of knowing his eternal damnation was mine to provide gives me a sense of peace. Hearing the last breath leave the chest of someone so inherently evil, I relish the penance it will take to combat this egregious failure in my task.

"Goodbye." I spin on my heel and turn toward the exit, when Bracken's voice carries across the space.

"Goodbye? The only thing you can say to your father is goodbye?" Yelling it questioningly, I can hear the pain lace each word. "How the fuck—"

"Brace!" one of the older men calls out.

"Don't, Sights!" Stomping away from Sights, his heavy jackboots rattle the floor. "This has nothing to do with you or the club, so kiss my fucking ass, old man. This has everything to do with my brother."

Coming to me, standing in my space, the fire breathes within Bracken as his hatred and sadness blends into a twisted sense of loyalty to a sick fucking example for a father. "Fuck you, Kyden. Fuck you and the pious bullshit you tout. Your God All-fucking-Mighty tasked you with sending souls onto the next world with compassion, penance, and fairness. Where is your fairness when you don't grant the final rites?"

"Bracken, you and I know better than all these men. He wasn't worthy of a path to God's gates. Hell's doors were *wide* open. They had a cool whiskey in hand and a pack of drunken whores lined up to suck his cock." After tonight, and the shameful words I've spewed, the gates have been opening up ever so slightly for me as well.

Laughing hard, Bracken's voice carries around the rafters. "Still a son of a bitch."

Standing toe-to-toe, the two of us are perfectly matched in size and height. I'll not give him the satisfaction of causing me further grief this night.

Turning, I walk away from him and the other deadened souls, calling over my shoulder, "Close the doors on your way out. I'd hate to let trouble enter into the house of God."

Chapter Seven

RETURNING TO MY RESIDENCE took longer than I'd hoped. Instead of returning straight away, I ventured out into the extensive gardens to take in God's beauty.

At night, the rich greens and once vibrant reds become muted. A white is cream, or a soft green becomes harsh and jagged. Red is black, exactly how my soul is at this moment—charred and tainted, without care, and not an ounce of compassion. He had no right to the steps of God's kingdom, right?

Sending Scarlet to *fetch me* was dirty and underhanded. It shouldn't surprise me that Bracken did it. He only does what's best for Bracken and the Bows.

Growing up as boys in the club, we saw, did, and learned far more than any other prepubescent adolescent should. By the time we hit ten, both of us had vetted out retribution to those who deserved to learn a valuable lesson. The lesson being, even a child can be dark and deceitful if trained correctly. My first tortured soul was before I even grew pubic hair. The second was smoother. The third, and the consecutive ones that followed were praised. It felt good to be wanted by the club. Until her.

DG knew that she was in our class at school. She'd only just transferred in a few months before, but she'd caught the eyes of the Madox boys. Her stockbroker parents worked in a high-stakes firm. DG thought that stocks would be a great front for filtering the profits of his seediest ventures. He didn't voice that to us, though. That was a secret until we were older. Being young men in a club didn't allow us entrance to club's church meetings, even if he was our father. We followed the requests as they were presented without question, hoping to one day gain entrance to the most sacred parts of the organization.

Knowing what the club was in to wasn't a secret, as everyone knew. Even our classmates knew that you didn't cross the Madox boys, or any member of the Broken Bows. We had a family behind us that would break the bones of anyone who did us wrong. Scarlet was naive to that life. Moving into the area, learning secondhand what club life and loyalty meant, Scarlet crossed paths with a few of the girls. Girls you *didn't* cross. With a nasty scar on her stomach to prove it, the valuable lesson was learned fast—*make us your friend.*

As a girl she was gangly, almost as tall as Brace and I, and could dish out honesty like a sharp blade. I fell in love, hard and fast. Sure, Bracken tried on more than one occasion to gain entrance to her well-guarded heart, but it was no use. We may look identical, but our demons are as different as a house cat is to a tiger. Sadly, both can be lethal to their prey.

She told me that she'd seen something in him that was too dark to redeem. Right then, I'd thought it was an odd response as we were the same in so many ways. Now, I understand the connotation. His demons blaze hot, never resting. Mine have cooled, no thanks to her.

On this one stinking, hot summer day, we were more interested in pools, beaches, and bikinis. DG requested us for a mission. Her parents were still pushing the club off, and they'd added security detail to Scar and themselves. With our access to her, he wanted us to remind them who ran the show in town.

As classes ended for the day, something was different. Normally, we'd walk her home with her detail hot on our heels. There was no detail. DG had us distracting her for a few hours to make her parents worry, just to scare them. But there was more to it. Unbeknownst to me, Bracken was in on a *special* plan. Passing one of the abandoned buildings we always walked by, Brace thought to detour through the wrecked shell. I thought we were only going to keep her away, no harm no foul. No.

"See that?" Brace asked.

She checked out the window he pointed to. "I don't see anything, Brace." His smirk told me that his dark angel had a plan brewing.

"Come on. We'll only be a few minutes. I swear I saw someone inside."

"There's always people in there, B. Let's just get home. My parents will wonder where I am," Scarlet stated, trying to walk away toward home.

Grasping her arm tight, Bracken was determined to make her go where he wanted. As always, I followed along. Never one to go against him, I followed without fault.

Trying to appease Brace and calm Scarlet's fears, I said, "Come on, Scar. It'll only be a few minutes. No one will be there. We'll go out the back door and make it home before anyone even knows we're missing."

Even then, Scarlet knew that she owned my heart. I might have been a malicious fuck, but I was hers from the start. Tall, dark perfection. Attitude to rival even us, never afraid to go toe-to-toe with girls if she felt they were wrong, and sassy sarcasm that would end an argument.

"Fine, but let's get out of here soon. Last thing I want is rabies." Taking my hand in one of hers and Bracken's in the other, the three of us walked into the dark building.

The dim light of day waned through the shattered windows, casting shadows on the floor. We'd never gone in there before, but it didn't stop us from wanting to explore it. At least, that's what I thought. Brace's idea was different.

Partially built mannequins were strewn around the area, looking like dismembered bodies after a war, with dirt covering the faces. Funny enough, a few had clothes on them. Someone had turned the space into an odd fashion show, lining them up and down in rows, with torsos laid out on the floor. With the heads just out of reach, it looked as if the arms were grasping for the rolling orbs. "Brace, this is creepy as shit. Can we just go, please?" Visibly bothered by the macabre scene, Scarlet started for the door. I found it was soothing in an unsettling way. Dead bodies were never an issue for me as I'd seen my fair share from an early age.

"Come on. You're not scared, are you, Scar? We're just going to have a little fun." Kicking the head closest, the noise bounced off the wall with a sickly clunk. Grabbing up a body, Brace moved around with his dance partner.

"Let loose, girl." Dropping the body, he pulled Scarlet into his arms and shifted her around the space.

Watching the two of them laughing, Scarlet finally started to have fun. Twirling, spinning back and forth toward Brace, her infectious laughter filled the space. I always found her laugh a perfect blend of sweet and innocent.

"B, you dance like shit."

"Do not. You have no rhythm, woman." Dipping quickly, her long hair swept the ground, disturbing the dust.

"I'll bet Kyden dances way better than you do."

"Not likely," I said, pulling up a seat on a somewhat clean bench as I watched them continue on.

Slowing down, moving to a different beat, Bracken's hands searched under Scarlet's shirt. Exploring her back, she peeled his hands down before he raised them again. Unclasping her bra, his steps ceased. Kissing her neck, pulling her in tight, his hands explored the front of her shirt as she protested.

"I'm not in for that, B. Stop." She tried to reattach her bra as she backed away. But he was stronger, and more determined.

"Let's have fun, shall we?" Pulling at the top, he lifted it up and dipped his head to suck on her tit. I watched in absolute wonder as her body stiffened, but his became driven by need.

"No, Bracken, don't do this. You'll regret it. Please," she pleaded as Bracken held her so tight that she couldn't refuse. Even as Scarlet tried to move away, I saw him become more determined. Holding her by the jeans with one hand and grasping her by the neck with the other, I wondered how far he would go.

To me, the milky brown skin of Scarlet was mesmerizing. Watching with a detached interest, only wondering what the rest of her body would be like, jealousy of his boldness coursed through me as I watched. I was a voyeur as he took what he wanted from her.

"Ky, aren't you going to join in?" Brace asked. Snapping me from my vacant musings, I looked to Scarlet. Her face showed pain, fear, and hope. Hope that I would help her.

We weren't naive when it came to women's bodies, and we never had to force someone into it. There was enough club pussy to slake anyone's needs. Being nearly sixteen, DG gave us each a present two months ago; a pair of club sluts to show us what it meant to be men. Even then, my cock was revved up as I watched what Bracken was doing to Scarlet.

The difference was that I'd always wanted it willingly from her.

"Bracken, let's go home. Scarlet doesn't want that, man."

"'Course she does. Don't kid yourself, she's always wanted us. Who *doesn't* want to fuck us? You do, don't you, Scar?" Unbuckling her jeans, he forced his hand in. Scarlet slapped him hard across the face.

"Fuck off, Bracken! I don't want you." Pushing hard against his chest, she stepped back. A blaze of fire screamed through Bracken's features.

"Tsk tsk. This is what happens when you go against the club. Tell your parents about this and it won't go any better on them. Don't you want your family safe, Scar? Give me what I want and I'll tell DG you were a good little cunt."

She looked at him in shock. "No, Bracken, don't do what DG wants." Pleading, tears fell down her cheeks. "We're friends. Don't do this."

"You don't get a choice. Now, do you want me in your cunt or ass? Either way, you get a Madox in you." Sneering darkly, Brace looked at me. "Come over here, brother. You get first choice if she doesn't choose. Front or back? We're test driving this model first."

Pressing his body into hers, backing her against a table, I watched with a sick fascination. Yes, I'd wanted her. Yes, she was all I thought about as I slapped my cock alone at night, but I'd never wanted her unwillingly. "No. I don't want—"

"Don't fucking lie to me! I know you, Kyden. You want her just as bad as I do. Right now, she has no choice unless she wants to be an orphan."

"No. Stop, Brace. Let's just go home. Tell dad a story, act like we did it. Leave her alone."

Laughing loudly, the proverbial screws pulled loose in his head. I knew when the darkness broke free and his demons overrode all his actions. There was no stopping Bracken.

"No way. I'm following through. You can leave now, ignoring her screams as I tear her apart, or you can stay and enjoy her sweet, virgin pussy." Yanking at her shirt, lifting it so that her arms were tied in, Bracken pushed her to lie down on the dusty, trash covered table.

"No, Bracken! No! Please, stop!" Fighting against him, Scarlet's cries fell on deaf ears.

He smacked her across the face, hard. "This'll go easier on you if you just relax and let it happen, yeah?"

My cock hardened as I watched. I felt horrible that it did. I'd wanted her ever since she'd arrived. My dreams and waking hours had been plagued with thoughts of what it would be like with Scarlet. Looking at me, pleading with her eyes to stop my brother, I turned and ran from the building. I never looked back.

Still thinking of that day, it reminds me of the reasons for entering the seminary and leaving our family *business.* In no way did I escape that moment in time unscathed. My heart and soul was never really theirs. I found no joy in the tunings, the shakedowns, or the scare tactics of the club. I just couldn't do it. Running away at seventeen, I ran straight into the arms of God and his teachings.

Do I believe it was best for me? Yes.

Do I believe all I did was trade one omnipotent being for another? Damn right I did.

Now, today, I've questioned every ounce of that decision. Running from them didn't get rid of the club, it just kept them in the background and gave them time to grow more powerful.

"Any room on the bench, Father?"

I don't turn. "Of course. Have a seat."

Shifting slightly, I give Scarlet room to sit beside me. "Do you want to talk about it?" she asks very calmly.

"Not really much to talk about. The man was a monster, but I should have done my job."

"Not true, Kyden." Pausing, she lets the pregnant air hold us in place where words aren't necessary. She agrees, but won't voice it aloud. Knowing well enough that our past clouds things, and that she's lady enough to sometimes let things lie doesn't help.

"You know," I say, "there are times I think of what my life would be like if I'd done what DG wanted, if I'd just gone along with everything."

"You know that you and Bracken might share the same genes, but you're a different man." Touching my hand gently, I feel the warmth of her skin. It soothes me.

"We're more alike that most know. Even you, Scarlet."

Smiling softly, her makeup shimmers slightly in the dim moonlight. "There's always been more to you than anyone knows."

Creeping her fingers up my wrist, gently touching a particularly sensitive scab, I move to pull away. "Don't pull away from me, Kyden."

"I don't pull away from you, Scarlet. I pull away from that life. I'm no longer that man. I'm a man of God. I'm a man of the cloth." I try to put up a convincing fight. Her touch elicits so many feelings.

"I saw the marks, Kyden."

"I know you did." I don't move her hand. I can't.

"Why do you do that?"

I can't answer. Nothing needs to be said about it.

"Can I see?" she asks.

Considering it, I lift the edge of my cassock, then the sleeve of my shirt. Revealing the various aged cuts, including tonight's, Scarlet inspects them wordlessly, feathering each of them, admiring them or feeling sorry for me. I'm not sure which, but I don't want her to stop.

"Kyden—"

I cut her off fast to remind her, or maybe more so myself. "*Father Kyden*, Scarlet. I'm a priest." Pulling my arm back, I push the cloth back down and rise from the seat. "I'm *your* priest."

"You're right. You're a priest, *Father* Kyden. But you're a man, starving for attention. I see it all the time. Every Sunday you stare at me. You're hungry, and you want to devour me. You look at me like a locust looking for a meal. Everything about you shows the cry for a need to be touched." Rising to stand behind me, Scarlet pushes up against me. Wrapping her arms around me unbidden, I fall into the touch. Closing my eyes, I revel in the scent of her. It's an aphrodisiac. In this garden, she should be the least powerful scent, but I take in her perfume as if the world is void of smells.

"Touching you is all I dream of. There's never been a moment when I didn't care about you, Kyden. It's always been you."

Touching her arm, I wish for nothing more than to stay wrapped up in her, but it's inappropriate for a parishioner and her priest. Pulling away, I turn around to face her, coming eye to eye with a woman my heart has belonged to from the day I met her. Everything falls away.

God, give me strength. I never should have turned around. Seeing those chocolate endless depths, they drag me in like Lot's wife. Looking at her, I understand the reference even more than biblically. Temptation is a hard truth to fight.

Raising my arm, I touch her face. My resolve bends and bows. "Scarlet, I—"

Pushing a finger up against my mouth, she says, "Kyden, you're a man with needs. You never took a vow of celibacy, did you?"

Shaking my head, Scarlet pulls her hand away. When she presses her mouth to mine, I'm shocked. Her lips are smooth, plump, and skillful as she gives me something no one has in years—compassion, and passion. I accept it. I feel that it's a sin to want it, but at the same time, she's right. I never vowed it to God. I only promised myself that it wasn't mine to covet.

Have I envied others for the passion they show in public? That they feel in private moments? I wish to enjoy that. I miss it like nothing else.

As Scarlet's tongue darts within my mouth, searching out, feeling for mine, a moan escapes me. Pulling back with the slightest amount of willpower, her name leaves my lips on a whisper, "Scarlet."

"Don't deny it further, please. I've wanted you for more time than I can admit, Kyden. Remove the stains of our past. Pull away the reminders of everything that's tainted my life. Give yourself to me." Reaching for my cock, Scarlet holds me in place with the tool of my demise.

Sucking in a deep breath, I stiffen at the contact. I've dreamt of nothing but this for so many years.

I silently vow, *Father Almighty, please understand I'll deny myself no more. I've decided to give myself to her.*

Standing in the reflection garden after my father's death is not what I had in mind for a moment such as this. "Not here," I tell her. Taking her hand in mine, Scarlet steps in pace beside me.

Moving as if the damned are on our heels, we reach the doors of my residency within seconds. We're like two teenagers. Before the door is even shut, we're on each other.

Watching as Scarlet undoes each button with care, she smiles up at me as she peels it over my head. My mind reels with all the thoughts I've tucked away for reference. Removing her heels and placing them by the door, she turns back and I look—really look—at the woman who has plagued me daily.

"You're all I ever think of, Scarlet. Every day, every moment, every second ticks down and you're on my mind. Release me now from this hell. Let me live in peace in my church. Leave. Never look back, never return. Give me up." Taking in her schooled features, she gives nothing away.

"I wish I could, but I can't. Truly, Kyden, I need you and I always have." Stepping close, she removes my clerical collar and sets it on the table by the door.

My body reacts with a will of its own, and I anticipate her at the wheel of this disaster.

"Kyden," she murmurs, pulling at the button on my trousers. I suck in a breath. It's tight, hot, and needy. As if I'm watching from afar, I gaze at the deftness of her touch while she lazily thumbs the top of my penis, the director of my blazing need. My cock is the commander of this. Breathing raggedly, my chest heaves with the need for her to grip me tightly, to treat me with disgust.

"Don't hold back," I tell her. "Treat me as if I'm a toy you wish to punish. Please."

Finally grasping it around the trunk, she squeezes it tightly.

"Like that, Kyden?"

"Fuck, yes. Just like that." Enjoying the tough tugs, she pulls harder, tighter. Pushing down with a roughness that I can't achieve on my own, I revel in the pain. When punishing myself, I grasp it hard, but I know when to quit, when to slow down, and when to push it a bit further. Her unknown is far more tantalizing. Moving hotly back and forth, I scratch at my arm through the thin shirt. The pain is necessary for my penance.

"Kyden?" she questions, pulling my hand away from my arm. "Do you need that too?"

How do I answer that? Do I tell her the need is to remove the sin from my tainted soul? She may leave, and I'll feel even dirtier. Taking a chance, I tell her the truth. It's Scarlet, after all. "Yes. It's a part of the penance for my transgressions. Yes, Scarlet, I have a driving need to punish myself." Blinking, acknowledging what I've told her, she stops her movements. Pulling her hand back, she steps away to the edge of the dead fire. Picking up the kit I left in a rush, she turns back.

Unfurling the frequently stained cloth, she unties it and inspects the tools of my repentance. Lovingly touching each blade, she walks back across the room with a smile on her face.

"Can I watch? Or can I participate? Is it the pain, or the anticipation of pain that excites you?" I'd never thought of it that way, but she sees something that I hide.

"I've only ever been alone. No one knows of it." Nodding her understanding, she selects a blade. It's one of my favorites. Twelve inches long, a thin boning knife blade. Honed to a sharpness that would slice off the head of my cock in a single swipe, the handle is bone, with all color worn off from use.

"Would this be okay?" she asks with trepidation. I don't think she's afraid to do it. I think she's afraid to take something from me that I relish.

"Yes."

Setting the rest of the set aside, she holds the handle reverently, as if it's a favored friend. "Strip," she commands.

"Scarlet—"

"Don't *Scarlet* me, Kyden. Strip." At her serious expression, I begin.

Pulling off my shirt, I then remove my trousers, boxers, and socks, and stand completely naked in my living quarters. Staring down the woman who holds my attention fully, she catalogues my scars.

"Kyden, that's a lot." Slightly covering myself, I'm fearful of her disgust. "Don't cover yourself to me." Touching my face, she raises my chin, her gaze showing only acceptance and care. "Never hide from me, Kyden."

Stepping close, her breath tickles the skin on my chest. I watch her with a tremendous amount of fear. Will she fear it? Will she run from this? After all, it is a lot.

"Scarlet, you don't have to—"

"I don't do things I don't want to. Do I, Kyden?" Thinking about it, she doesn't. No one has ever been able to control her. Sure, Bracken tried to, but nothing broke her, nothing halted her forward motions. Scarlet is a lone soul that depends on no one.

Looking down, inspecting the newest cuts on my legs, Scarlet touches them with her finger. "Does it hurt?"

Even as she feathers the damage, my cock pulses with need and I groan. "No. It isn't pain I need. It's the absolution of my daily transgressions."

"What was it that caused this today?" She's truly curious. I'm amazed at her interest.

"I was tempted by the devil. To love, to act upon my need to father children. To show them love and giving them a home."

"Giving an unwanted child a home or fathering children isn't a sin, Kyden." She's confused by my reasons.

"No. But wanting what is not mine is. Wanting and envying others for what they so flatly don't care for or appreciate is not as valiant."

Scraping a nail along the inside of my leg, almost touching, yet missing anything sexual is tantalizing. "So, you coveted what was not yours to want?" She understands it better than I thought she would have. "You were jealous?"

"Yes. One of the deadliest sins. 'Those who practice envy and strife are barred from the kingdom of heaven.' Cain, Joseph, and their brothers. Are there not purer examples of how envy destroys us all?"

"You would know better than I, Father." Placing the knife along the soft flesh of my left leg, Scarlet drags the length of it across without breaking skin.

Holding my breath, my chest tightens and my cock stiffens to the point of pain as the scabs pull apart. "Fuck," I say aloud.

"Tell me what you need, Kyden."

Gripping my cock in hand, I slowly stroke it.

She stops me. "No, Kyden. I told you to tell me, not to do it yourself."

Releasing my grip, I pull back and look into her heated gaze. She's always been on my mind, and now she's here. It's wrong in so many ways, but I can no longer stop it. All these years, she's the one that I've imagined being here with me.

"Touch me. Cut me. Just being here is painful and excruciatingly perfect."

"Fine. But you tell me, you don't touch. Understood? Otherwise, I'll leave and take your instruments with me." Waiting for my response, she pulls the blade back and grasps my cock, tight. "Do you understand me, Kyden?"

"Yes! Yes, I understand, Scarlet."

"Good." Smiling smugly, her eyes twinkle with mischief. "Now, tell me what you need."

I motion like I do before every repentance. "Forgive me Father, for I have sinned. Today I coveted the need for a family, allowing jealousy and envy within my soul. Please, accept my absolution." Scarlet watches intently as I move through the motions. "Please, place the towel on the floor." Kneeling down, I wait for her to do as instructed.

Setting the boning knife on the table nearby, she places the towel in front of me. Pulling it closer, I lay it just under my knees. I rise up so that my back is ramrod straight. "Come down here."

Tucking her flowing skirt between her knees, she kneels directly across from me. Reaching over, I grab the knife and hand it to her. I'd never noticed until now that I treat it like something as important as a limb to an amputee. Without it in its place, anxiety creeps up my spine.

"Would you touch me? I've always imagined it was you touching me."

Kneading her brows together, she reaches forward, grasping my cock loosely.

"No, not like that." Placing my hand across hers, I tell her, "Like this. It's penance. More painful than pleasurable."

"Okay, Kyden." Tightening her grip, she squeezes with a strength I never thought she owned. It excites me.

"Yes!" Admonishing myself for the outburst, I say in a softer tone, "Yes. Like that, please."

Stroking slowly at first, the feel of her soft hand pulling and pushing to a beat of her selection is erotic as hell.

"Is this good?"

"Yes, it is." I turn my outstretched, scarred right arm out toward her. "Cut me. I need it."

Switching hands, she adjusts to produce the same pressure as before. Groaning out at the tension, she looks into my eyes. "You're sure, Kyden?"

"Absolutely. Please," I plead.

Accepting the driving force I have, Scarlet places the knife against the raised, punished skin. Sliding it across, I feel the exhilaration that I do every time the blade separates skin. "Yes, that's right. Pump my cock as hard as you can."

Gaining speed, Scarlet pulls the knife against the skin again. Seeing the blood dribble off my dark skin, my heart sinks and sings all at once. "Father, forgive my sins." But the building pressure hasn't dissipated. My sins haven't been absolved. More is needed. My sins must be great for defaulting on my vow to assist all souls to the gates of Heaven. No. I don't believe that. He didn't deserve entrance, but the choice to choose wasn't mine to decide at time of death. That was my God's to decide.

The foundations of my faith have been severely shaken today. Placing my hand on the handle of the knife, I stop her hand. "On the leg."

Without asking further, Scarlet turns the handle low. Inspecting the shallow cuts along the inner soft flesh, she selects a clean spot. It's not that it's untouched territory, but it's been a long time. The scars there are a deep brown. Clasping the blade tightly, coursing it from my knee toward the groin, I feel further relief.

Scarlet must know she's helping give me something that no one ever has. This is a peace I couldn't fathom explaining if I was asked. Moving quicker now, pulling the scabs apart, I relish the punishment.

Scarring my leg again and again, purposefully thrusting her hand with a damaging stroke, I groan.

"More. Faster." I arch my back to the pain. "Don't stop," I shout out as the pressure builds. Closing my eyes, accepting the tearing heat, I don't at first feel a change. Moving low, covering the head with her mouth, Scarlet sucks my cock deep within. The heat is tremendous and almost indescribable. Thrusting my hips forward, Scarlet strikes my skin again with the blade. Faster than ever before, my release creeps up and spills forth, down her throat.

Crying out, the pleasure mounts as my blood flows down my leg. As my seed spills into Scarlet's sweet mouth, my hips rock with a will of their own.

Calming my breathing as the orgasm ends, she releases me from her mouth and licks her lips.

"That was interesting, Kyden." Pulling the towel off the floor, she hands it to me before setting the knife on the kit.

Cleaning the surface of the knife, I lovingly slip it into its holster before patting down the freshly made scars on my leg and arm.

Rising off the floor and straightening her outfit out, I watch in absent interest. Sex with another is something that I never thought would happen again. No, it wasn't intercourse, but there was an intimacy that I felt was lost to me for life.

"Could I trouble you for a glass of water?" she asks sweetly.

I'm sure the taste of me in her mouth must be potent and unfriendly. "Of course." Lifting off the floor, I grab my clothes and dress quickly before walking off to the kitchenette. "I'm not sure what to think of this, Scarlet," I say as she waits in the living area.

I pour her a glass of water from the faucet and make my way back to the living room. Surprised to find we're no longer alone, a quick understanding courses through me.

Chapter Eight

TAKING IN THE UNWANTED guest, my blood heats with fury. "Why are you here?"

"Hello to you too, *brother*. After such a trying night, I expected you to be cordial." Handing the drink to Scarlet, I notice that her demeanor has changed.

Speaking to my brother, I try to avoid the obvious setup. "Bracken, one would assume you'd knock before entering a person's residence."

Crossing the room, he takes a seat in the chair and plunks his feet up on the hearth, commanding the space in a dark and despicable way.

"Well, brother, I thought we could have that conversation again about you returning to the club."

With a melancholic stare, I inspect the position Scarlet takes beside my brother. She's upset, but not in the way I'd expect. "What would you like, Bracken?"

"We have an opportunity in the club, and with the recent events—"

"Events being that your leader is dead." Crossing my arms across my chest, I try to hide the fresh scars. Bracken rises from the chair, pissed.

"You know, *Father,* I feel you owe the club now. After all, you didn't complete the task set forth by your God." He glides his tongue along his teeth. "You're a poor excuse for a priest if you ask me, Father Kyden."

"Not my problem. I'm absolved by *my God*. I've atoned for my sins tonight."

"Ah." He points to Scarlet. "Yes. Let's address that." Tromping around the small space, touching small trinkets here and there, he says, "How was it again that you atone, Father Kyden?"

"Through the needs of my confession. My confession is my own and personal, *brother.*" If this is going where I think it is, I'm in a heap of trouble.

Clapping his hands, the evil grin he gives enlightens me to the full scale of the activities of his machinations of tonight.

"I see you get it. Bravo. At least I don't have to explain it to you, Kyden." Stepping toward Scarlet, he places his arm around her waist and kisses her full on the mouth, passionately.

Breaking away and moving toward the door arm in arm, I see the extent of my mistake. She was a tool of my demise as much as I was to myself.

"We'll be expecting you at the clubhouse within the week, Father."

"And if I decide to ignore your request?" I ask flatly.

"You can't."

"Oh, I'm sure I can."

Laughing darkly, he pulls the door partially closed after Scarlet exits. "Your current skills will be immeasurable, and your past skills will be accepted with open arms, *Strike*."

Leaving with a crass clunk of the door, I stand immobile in the center of my room, shocked and pissed off at what I let happen tonight.

Chapter Nine

LAST NIGHT, MY OWN activities, the outcome, and the derisive decision created a sleepless night. With my brother's unwelcome invitation, my mind was scattered and seething with anger. Even the thought of a further atonement caused disgust in my actions. Tucking my tools away in a cupboard, I wept. For a while, I was unsure of how I would find peace, of how I could face my parishioners as their cleric as the Godly ambassador. My heart was extra heavy.

Leaving after my brother and Scarlet, I exited my small cottage and returned to the chapel. Finding it devoid of any reminders of DG's poorly enacted funeral rites, I slumped down in the front pew. Staring up at the Christ on the cross, I considered my overall performance as of recent.

"Forgive me, Father. I've represented you in an ungodly light. How can I ask others to repent and refrain from repeating their sins if I, as their priest, cannot do the same? I've never doubted that my position was here, that the Bows had no need for me. But am I any different than their executioner ways? Have I really condemned a man to the gates of Hell because I couldn't refrain from letting my past cloud my image of him? Will he be stuck in purgatory because I couldn't send him to be judged? Did I really hate him that much?" Asking question after question, no answer came. Did I expect that he'd answer me, granting me the wisdom after my sick performance as his representative?

"Tell me how to fix this? *Can* I fix this? What can I do, Father? Guide me."

Sitting alone in the chapel, taking in the motion of the light as it danced across the stained-glass frescoes that line the halls, I watched the sun rise without an answer.

As morning arrived, so did the parishioners. Their needs and wants were above any of mine, so accepting their confessions became a driving need. As the morning wore on, I gave them more leniency than I normally would have, but with a heavy heart. How could anything else be expected?

Sitting in the confessional, awaiting another repentant, I'm melancholic. Hearing the door beside me open and the shutter slide closed instead of open, I know the person next to me wishes to be unknown in every way.

"Father?"

"Yes. How may I help you today, son?"

"It's not how you can help me, but how I can help you."

Taken aback by the man's response, I wait for further explanation.

"You see, I know of some pictures that are circulating today." The man sits back against the stiff wood, just as someone from the outside slips an envelope through the base of my door. Picking up the plain case, I open it and find a small stack of transgressions. They're not just from last night, either. They're current selections of my penance ritual in my residence, the day I stroked out one with Scarlet in the very seat the man now sits, and of course last night. Seeing Scarlet's mouth on my cock with her hair spilling over, my pants tighten unbidden.

"Fuck!" I say, a little louder than I should. I select the tattered, stained, and faded picture of a past I thought dead.

Regaining my composure, I pocket the pictures and ask what he undoubtedly is waiting to hear. "What do you have to gain from this?"

"Father, forgiving sins is only one part of the job. There's many things that a man in your position can help...accommodate."

Understanding his request, I curse myself for the position I've put myself in. "What accommodations are expected? I'm not naive, but I still need further leading before I'll accept any blackmail worthy of my eternal soul."

"Bows bend, not break, Father." Rising from the seat, he opens the door and the light streams in, showcasing his leather cut. "We'll be in touch."

With the door closing quickly behind him, I'm given no chance to respond.

Chapter Ten

LEAVING, AS IF MY CASSOCK was on fire, I gave directives to the Sisters that I was unwell, and that the duties of the day were in their control.

Reaching my cottage, I strip off my outfit in a manner unlike any other time. The ritual of care has been lost. I dress in civilian clothes that I keep at the back of my closet. Most of them are dusty and lacking in care, but it makes no difference. Grabbing my wallet, lacing my boots and grabbing the pictures, I leave the house and property as fast as I can. I need to get away, as far as humanly possible. In essence, stripping off the better parts of me and leaving the darkness to take back what it never released.

For the past ten years, I've hid the evil man inside the wardrobe of a saint. The pictures today reminded me that you cannot escape your past. With no real direction or care, I let my body lead me as it wished. Pulling down past the rundown row housing, the odd person greets me with a shocked stare and gaping jaw.

"Now, now, I know you're out of your element, *Padre*." The young black punk, Conry, sneers at me, showcasing his gold capped teeth. "What are you doin' around here? No one needs blessings." He swings around his baggies of crank. "I got what they need to escape their sins."

Walking on, I ignore him and his small-time street thugs. "Blessings and confessions aren't on my mind today, Conry." I'm not the police, and right now, I'm not even their priest.

"Suits me fine. Have a nice day, sir." He snickers as his friends all laugh at his quip.

Moving along, I can still hear him making snide remarks, but I don't care. To be honest, I feel every bit of tension leave me. It's been resting on my shoulders over the past, the current, and it certainly will into the future. Have I ever been enough?

Absently tracing the scars on my arm, the pain of the current marks give me more determination to follow through with my plan. I'm not sure when it formed or solidified, but it's in place now. Nothing will stop me.

The day is clear, cool, and crisp. It may smell like despair and homeless shoes, but to me it's perfect.

Step after step, I think of the fucking pictures.

Fucking Bracken and his taunting need to bring me back to the family. "Well, you want me, brother, you should be wary of what you'll receive. Not all news is good, and not all gifts are wanted," I say aloud.

My steps are sure, and my mind is clearer than it has been in a long while. I hope that this decision is the correct one. There are no fears, no trepidation in my steps, no unnecessary second-guessing of my decision. This is right.

"Forgive me, Father, for I am about to sin."

God help them. God help them all for what they wrought upon themselves.

Chapter Eleven

COMING UP ON THE CLUBHOUSE, I see that nothing has changed in all these years. I've not stepped onto this street since I left. Never once did I think of it as a place I needed to visit again.

The chain link and brick is solid, yet aged. The gates are manned by young recruit members, holding it still as bikes rumble by. The sound of custom exhaust choppers are revving in the yard as they tune them, fix them, and prepare them for a ride.

In the yard, there are a few dark SUVs and vans for transports. One of them I suspect carried DG to my chapel less than twenty-four hours previously where his blood spilled across the bare metal of the floor, his life leaching out. Do I hate that he's gone? No, I don't. But I'm almost disappointed that he won't be here to see me do this, to see me walk through these doors.

Stepping up to the gates, the youngster manning it does a double take. Looking to his friend holding the other side, he shrugs his shoulders, clearly in as much confusion as his counterpart. Unsure of what to do, the two of them wave me in.

The yard looks no different to me. There are grease stains on the ground, brick and mortar holding the plain unassuming gray building together, and the garage on the side has the door high in the rafters as bikes are worked on.

There are bikers, cock bunnies, old ladies, daughters, sons, and babies playing at the dirty playground that Marksman set up for us when we were little. My memories and my fears are tied up in this building. Today, the fears are muted and the strength of determination is riding high. They shouldn't have fucked with me.

My monsters have been simmering in the background, held at bay by God's teachings, my preposterous repentance ritual, and the idea that I was a better person than them. Handing me the pictures—*that* picture—cracked open the gates of hell that have been inching wider day by day.

Striding across the grounds, the odd person stops what they're doing to watch me, whether in confusion like the two at the gates, or in recognition. It doesn't matter. I'm here with a hellish purpose.

Looking at the building, taking in the crest of my corruption, the symbol pulses with the fear of what I'm here to do. The blood red eyes of a buck skull struck through the center, pierced by an arrow as a crossed set of bows back its antlers, I read the motto beneath it, 'Blessed is the Arrow that Strikes True.'

My heart was never here, but my blackened soul was born of this building, this lifestyle, and this one percenter don't-give-a-fuck mentality. Quint started this club and he raised his sons to be the successors to the hierarchy.

Tugging on the door, the light of day seeps into the dank windowless space. Men rest at the bar top, drowning their sorrows in cheap bourbon and beer. Women sit across their laps, hoping for a bit of fun, or crowd the various couches that litter the edges of the space. Nothing at all has changed. Debauchery, disregard of women, overindulgent fucks and cocksuckers that only wish to ride or die.

Letting my sight adjust to the dim light, I let the door close behind me with a bang. A few turn, but most keep on with their own needs. Searching out the space, the first person I'm looking for is the asshole who brought me the pictures. Finding him resting along the side wall with his feet propped up on the edge of the pool table, I smile. Rising, he grins a sickly grin that tells me he knew I couldn't resist showing up.

Turning a nod his way, I keep looking for Bracken. Tried and true, he sits to the side in DG's chair, king over all, keeping an eye on the rabble. A woman rests her head between his legs, bobbing up and down, sucking him deep. His head is rested back on the top of the chair as he holds her head in place. If she can breathe, it's a fucking miracle. *Me* swearing, even in my own mind is a miracle. But if they wanted Strike, they got him.

Turning, I find what I only halfheartedly expected to find. A sick happiness courses through my demon. Touching the edge of the shaft, I read out the inscription, 'Wild and True.' Petting it like I do my favorite knife, the soul of it sings its joy of being with its master once more. Pulling it off the rack, taking down my quiver and a selection of flights, I feel excitement. Notching a mark, drawing the arrow, the target has no idea that he's the one I'd thought of the whole way over here. Swinging back to the pool table, I find the big bastard oblivious. Releasing, the feel of the string reverberating the draw in my hand is like a heavy breath being expelled. The weight of tension in my shoulders is twenty pounds lighter, my neck is fluid and relaxed, and my jaw lets out a single click of relief.

I don't turn to see the arrow hit its mark; I know it was perfect. "Ahhh!" he yells and the room stills. Parker Grane, known as *Single Miss*, now has an arrow lodged in his right shoulder, holding him to the wall he was leaning against. Notching a second, I aim it straight at my brother.

I yell out his road name. "True!" His eyes slowly open, like he was expecting a show such as this.

Tapping the woman in his lap, she lifts her head. The mass of curls sling back to show a young girl of no more than eighteen. Dragging a thumb across her lips, she rises off the floor, stalking to the side.

"Strike. Good to see you, brother." Moving to lift out of the chair, I cock another arrow. Releasing it fast, it lands to the right of his face.

"Stay there. We're not talking."

Tipping his head to the side, he touches the feathers of my custom arrows. He knows how much that irks me.

Out of the corner of my eye, I watch as SM cracks the shaft to release himself from the position I left him in. A few of the men stop their game to assist him, while others grab up their pistols. Without turning, I shake a finger at them, to alert them that I'm watching their every move.

"Oh, we're talking, Strike. I don't think you came all this way just to put holes in the members then leave without a conversation." Lifting out of the chair, he pulls the arrow out and sets it on the bar top, lovingly.

"Maybe I came for my toys."

He laughs. "Doubt that. Come on. We'll go to the old man's off—*my* office." Correcting himself, he turns to the bar and picks up two bottles of beer. "Come. It's not blessed wine, but it'll do in a pinch." Not looking to see if I join, he walks off, popping the caps on the bottles as he moves.

Slipping the quiver and bow across my shoulder, I tromp off after Brace.

The door to the office is the first in the hall. Stepping inside, Bracken takes a seat in the chair, slugging back a good helping of his beer. Setting the other in front of where I'm to sit, Bracken motions for me to take a seat.

"Consider this reverse confession, Father. I'll tell you what I want and you do the penance."

Laying the bow in the spare chair, I sit. Before leaving the church today, I had no misgivings that I'd be sinning in some form, or two. I pick up my beer. "In for a penny, in for a pound, right?"

"That's right." Clinking the bottle neck to mine, Bracken smiles. It's sweet, something that I thought was lost. Maybe even a psychopath can have a good smile.

Sipping back on the fermented concoction, I relish the cool bubbles as they work their way down. "Tell me what you want, Bracken. You always have a plan. Two to three steps ahead, so this has been coming long before DG was shot the other night."

Pursing his lips, he nods. I know that look. He knows I see through his shit. We're of the same cut, cloth, and genes.

"I need a front. Our crank is being intercepted. It's time you used that church of yours for something good."

Okay, I expected something of me, but that? "No! No fucking way, Brace. You're not using the—"

"Look, we'll compensate the church. You'll get a new roof, new pews, the stained glass can be upgraded and no one will know you're a cutter that covets what he can't have."

Absently touching the fresh scars, the fear I had coming here is now a fire burning to tear this place down, brick by brick, motorcycle gear by gear. I've heard enough.

"No." Rising, I slam the beer on the table. "Fuck you, the devil you rode in on, and the wings of the demon that bred us." Grabbing up the arrows and bow, I start for the door.

"Don't you want to know about the picture? About Scarlet after the other night?"

I halt. He's said the one name that is my weakness. I'm pissed that I fell for his evil workings.

"What do you want to tell me? Fucking spill it, Brace." Tossing me his phone, I turn it over. Pressing play, I watch.

Shuffling feet across a dirty floor, the camera pans until Scarlet comes into focus. Bound, gagged, and naked, she's strapped to a chair with her legs splayed wide. The tears stain her makeup. Her usually perfect hair is nappy with dirt and bits stuck here and there. The voices of various men can be heard in the background as they converse about who will go next. An obvious bruise is just rising on her cheek, and her breasts show bite marks. Stopping the feed, I throw the phone across the room and it smashes to pieces.

"Struck that final chord, have we? So will you do as we need, *Father*?"

My blood beats in my ears, drumming a heavy tune of hatred, retribution, and vengeance. A dark sinister laugh escapes me. It's a sound I didn't even think I could make. "Do as you want. You'll be punished as you punish others. Vengeance and blood."

"Oh, brother, no. Your punishment. You'll be the one receiving, not vetting it out."

"Well, we'll see." Stalking from the room, I can hear his laugh as I reach the doors and exit into the light.

Chapter Twelve

"KYDEN?"

Storming out of the clubhouse, my mind is on nothing more than anger. Anger for allowing my brother to engage me in a way that my temper has taken over the reins, and anger for falling prey to his will. Seeing Scarlet striding toward the clubhouse in a drop-dead outfit and that same bruise peeking out from under her makeup just adds fuel to the fire.

"No, Scarlet!" I sneer. Flames lick every nerve in my body right now, and the last thing I need is *her*.

"Kyden..." Her voice is soft and sweet. "I'm sorry for everything. Will you let me explain?"

It really doesn't matter the reason. We've always been, and always will be, wrong for each other. "There's nothing to explain, Scarlet. You and I are just tools of the Bows—always have been, always will be. Do yourself and me a favor. Don't return to the church. I don't want see you again." My words are cutting, like a sharp blade. I feel bad, but it's a harsh truth. Seeing her more will cause me further heartache.

"Kyden, I didn't have a choice."

"That's my point, Scarlet. We've *never* had a choice. I've been running from this club and it drags me back when it wants me. It's a noose around my soul." As much as I've tried to think differently, there's *never* been an escape.

Adjusting the bow up my shoulder, Scarlet advances toward me with sadness coating her features. "Don't!" I snap, backing away like a wounded animal. Stepping around her, I quicken my exit and leave the compound. Human contact is the last thing I need right now. Right now, I'm a taut bow ready to release the arrow at its target. One poorly said word, one quick move against me and I'll fire, dragging all those around me down.

To hell and brimstone. My soul is blazing in it right now.

<u>BRACKEN</u>

"Follow him," I tell SM. "Don't let my brother out of your sight. You understand me?"

"Got it, boss."

As Single Miss leaves, I rest back on the bar stool and toy with the flight of the arrow that Kyden left behind. I wanted to shock the piety out of him and blast that goodness out so badly, all for my own purposes.

"Come back to me, brother."

Chapter Fourteen

NOTHING IS AS OBVIOUS as a dangerous man walking out of a clubhouse dripping in blood. That's how I feel. My need to tear it down as God's archer, to destroy and redeem those that are standing against him is driving and painful. My chest heaves, my lungs seer, and my arms shake as I wish nothing more than to go back and finish what I'd started. Scarlet didn't help. The brief conversation made me want to burn it all down faster.

Tromping down the street, my footfalls are heavy and quick. The calm, cool priest that entered Sunday mass with a renewed sense of hope and happiness has now been left behind. In his place is the youth that stormed out of the clubhouse at seventeen with a reason to find a place opposite of his raising.

Quint wasn't a bad father. He didn't beat us, but he did mold us to be the instruments of death that he wished for his club in the future. Bracken is the son he wanted. He was the trident ready to impale enemies. I'm the failure to Quint's machinations. I was meant to be Strike. I was forceful, I was perfection, and I was the one he was proud of, until I left. Quint had nothing more to do with me after that day. And whether it was a father's pride for me defying him, or because he had no care for Christ, it mattered not. I was out. I was left alone.

Now Bracken is dragging me back because he hasn't changed. Everything is to better the club in his mind.

Scratching the skin of my arm, I relish the itch, the burn, and the tearing. Right now, the need to repent and mete out punishment is overwhelming. Everything I've seen in the past is disgusting, tainted, and tortured by the paintbrush of the devil. Passing the same rundown tenements, Conry and his boys are outside. Dealing in drugs, pushing it to the community, just like the Bows. My anger increases tenfold.

"Father Kyden!" It's said with an edge of malice and contempt. My name on his lips is a catcall to my damaged soul.

The church has always been a sanctuary, a place of peace, and now I don't belong there anymore. One simple moment in time adjusted too much. The wall that held the *good* within and the bad out has broken off. The bad is free now. The evil is tantalizing and whirling around me like smoke. The thick tendrils are palpable. I wish to cause mayhem and destruction. Walking on, trying to ignore them, I see Conry's mouth move, but the words are muted and unnecessary. I don't answer him. I can't. Unfortunately, I'm beyond redemption. Passing by them, yanking on my quiver, Conry tries to gain my attention.

Dismounting the bow from my shoulder, notching an arrow before it registers, I loose. Slamming into the chest of my mark, Conry's eyes widen in surprise.

"What the fuck..." is the last thing he says as his body slumps to the ground, dead.

My mind reels with the realization that I just took a life. The young man, though misguided and wayward, has just had his life snuffed out by my actions.

"You just shot him!" one of the other young men screams out.

As another bends down to check him, more and more of them snap at me, completely awestruck that I'd do such a thing. I'm not.

That was my gift. That was what DG had harnessed within me; the need to strike first and ask questions later. He'd given me and Bracken nicknames that suited our souls, not road names that were because of the club. We were his direct heirs. We were to strike fear and vet out the truth. Bracken could see into a man's soul at a young age and tell right away what the truth was, way before you wanted to give it. He knows the truth of me. I've been in hiding, trying to hold at bay my true nature.

Pulling away from the dead boy on the ground, I bless him out of habit. "In the name of the Father, and of the Son, and of the Holy Spirit. Amen." Rising, I shoulder my weapon of death and saunter off down the road, toward the house of the Lord. I'm no longer looking for repentance and forgiveness.

I'm now looking for retribution.

Chapter Fifteen

RETURNING TO THE CHAPEL, I'd let the good Sisters know that their duty for the day was over. I asked the remaining parishioners to leave nicely, of course, after tidings and blessings upon each were vetted out. It's not their fault I'm this way, and it's not theirs to deal with. No one will be the wiser of what was about to befall their priest.

Locking the doors to the chapel and walking into my cottage, I grab up a notepad and pen to write out letters. Whoever finds them first can divvy them out accordingly. I address each: Bracken, Scarlet, the Bishop of our district, and one to the parents of the boy I'd just murdered. Lovingly, I set them at the hearth.

Pulling out my kit, I then dress in my cassock, cleric's collar, and tidy up my cottage, making sure the space is neat for the next man to hold office here. I'm not naive, I've killed. I'm no longer in a position of holding this office for the faithful and dependent souls requiring a penitent man. Selecting two arrows, beautifully formed and matched, I shoulder the bow and grab up my kit.

Every step I take is heavy and with worth. I'll enter the house of God one last time and await my penance dutifully. Reaching the door to the chapel, but not quite entering, I hear my name.

"Kyden. Nice shot today."

Not turning, my pace toward my fate stays true.

Ignoring him, he continues on. "Kyden, we need to talk."

Pulling up short of grabbing the handle, I turn. Calmly, I say, "We're not talking, Parker."

"Well, we are. Don't open the door just yet."

"Look, I've done terrible things today and—"

"I know. I saw the boy." Coming closer, his demeanor is sorrowful. "And I don't think your brother will be disappointed. On the contrary, you'll be protected and cherished."

"That's the problem, Parker. Protection isn't necessary. Go back to the clubhouse and forget you saw me."

Rubbing his shoulder, I doubt he's dealt with his damage yet. Under his cut, the blood still coats the edge of his shirt, staining it. "Kyden, I can't."

"Look, I get that Bracken probably told you on pain of death to make sure I came back, but I'm not returning."

Shaking his head, he laughs. "Yeah, he said something like that."

Great. Give me another regret on top of my already compounded stack. "Sorry, Parker. My soul can't be responsible for more." Walking away, I leave him there, wondering how he'll get me to go.

Throwing open the door, I say again, "Go back, Parker. I'm not your problem."

"Oh, but you are. You just don't know why it's yours."

Chapter Sixteen

THE SILENCE IS DEAFENING in here. God's house is devoid of his intervention in this moment.

I listened to everything Parker had to say, and by the time he left, he understood that my needs and his wants aligned. Locking the door behind me so that I won't be interrupted, I'm happy about the outcome.

"Thank you, Father." Listening, my dead voice echoes off the empty hall. Even the lack of further sound tells me how I've been left to my own devices in his home. God knows I'm on the righteous path.

As my feet clack on the wooden floors, I continue on to the end of the hall. Reaching the font, I dip my fingers into the water and recite it for the last time. "In the name of the Father, and of the Son, and of the Holy Spirit. Thank you, Father, for hearing my sins. I look to atone for the damages done to others, for the sins of the flesh, for the sin of taking another life. For taking your name in vain, and for being a horrible guide to your flock. Please accept my penance as payment in full."

Unhooking my bow, I set the first arrow and loose it to the high wall. Knocking the second into place, I know this is right. God guided my arrows true.

Grabbing up my tattered and well-loved kit, I move off to the rear stairs that lead to the choir mezzanine. My heart is free. Setting it on a pew, everything feels right.

Opening the string that holds the towel, I toss it to the side. It won't be needed. Unrolling the kit, I run my fingers over the knives. Stopping at the worn boning knife, I leave it in its place. "You'll never be touched again." Instead, I glide my finger down the serrated, ten-inch blade, with hardly a drop of blood that's touched it. I'm pleased with the selection. Leaving my bow beside it, I finish the walk to the stairs and stride up.

Removing my cassock and cleric collar on the way up, I drop them to the ground and roll up the edges of both my sleeves. With each step on the worn stairs, I count down each penance. "Father, I've taken a life. The young man was broken and unrepentant, but he'd never had the chance to correct his mistakes." Cutting my arm, I watch the blood splat to the floor. "Please, forgive me for my sin."

Travelling slowly, I'm excited that this pain is almost over. "Father, I've allowed the sins of the flesh to taint my love for you and your teachings. Scarlet was my first love—my only love—and she was the one that tempted me at every stage of my life." Cutting my arm again, more blood seeps forth.

The remainder of my sins don't require verbal condemnation, but the cuts are deeper and more pronounced.

I'm not looking to survive this. Each cut is dealt in a way to assist in weakening my body and strengthening my resolve. Reaching the top of the stairs, stripping off my shirt, the blood seeps faster the more I move.

Removing two ropes from around the edge of the choir guardrail, I tie them off against the sturdiest point. Testing the strength of it, pulling it tightly, I'm sure that my work will hold. Cutting two further deep lines in my arms, the red leaves deep furrows that showcase the tendons and muscle. It's painful to wrap the ropes, but I deserve every bit of pain. Tightening the ropes in place, I say, "Forgive me, Scarlet. Of all those things I coveted, I had hoped you would be mine. Jealousy now has no room in my heart. Bracken, I envied your ability to walk through this life as you were intended. I'm sorry I could never walk with you.

"Thank you for accepting my penance, Father." Taking a deep breath, I sit on the edge and score the final lines into my skin. "In the name of the Father..." are the last words I speak before stepping off.

Chapter Seventeen

<u>BRACKEN</u>

Single Miss returning to the clubhouse without my brother, my twin, pissed me off. Sending him off to the medic, Josie, I left and rode as fast as I could to the chapel on the hill.

Scarlet insisted on coming with me, hoping that the two of us could talk some sense into Kyden. I assumed his pious ass would call the authorities, involving the police. That's the last thing the big bastard should do. He should know by now that I'd always welcome him back with open arms. Nothing he could ever do would stop me from bringing his ass home.

The ride over was a little longer than I wanted, seeing we had to detour around the murder scene, but I was damn fucking proud of Kyden. Strike had returned. Exceptionally, Kyden had returned more elegantly than I could've imagined.

Parking the bike, I walk to his tiny fucking shack at the back of the chapel and find the door unlocked. No real surprise, but the lack of activity around the chapel is. SM had warned me that Kyden had dismissed everyone and emptied out the parish, but the place is deathly quiet. Walking in, there's was no trace of him.

"Where is he? Fuck. What the hell did you do, brother?"

Stepping around me, Scarlet ventures directly to the hearth. Lying there are four letters neatly addressed. "Here, this is for you." Handing me the one, I stare at it.

His handwriting was always neat. I touch my name on the front, as it was written with love and care. Peeling it open, I read the contents. Every word spews bullshit and rhetoric about family, honor, and obligation to the church.

Reaching the end, I'm positive that he's done something stupid. Looking to Scarlet as she reads hers, the same is apparent in the way tears stream down her face.

Without waiting to hear what she's about to say, I run out of his residence as fast as humanly possible to the chapel. Reaching the back door, I find it locked tighter than a virgin's pussy. Tugging on it a few good times, it doesn't budge.

"Fuck! Kyden, open this goddamn door!"

With no answer, I unholster my piece and shoot the lock a good ten times before the strong wood releases its hold. Shouldering it again and again, it finally gives.

"Kyden! Where the fuck are you!" I run through the rear and into the main room. My heart pounds. My need to find him is so strong, I forget to breathe.

Seeing the mess he's made, everything else falls away. "No! Don't do this to me. No! Kyden, no, no!"

Hitting the stairs, I take them two or more at a time, reaching the top as fast as I can. Coming upon the tight bindings that hold him in place, I yank with all my might. A gut-wrenching scream fills the air and I know that Scarlet has joined me in this macabre moment. Her sadness pales in comparison to mine.

"Help me! Please." My voice booms off the walls as I wrench as hard as I can. Slowly inching him back, it's not enough. Fuck it.

"Scarlet, I'm cutting these. Help guide him down," I yell as I attempt to work him free. Fucking asshole made sure it was secure, tying it off at least three times on the sturdy benches. With his added weight, nothing moves, so I go for the gun again. "Come here. I need you up here now!" Her feet bound off the stairs, clicking fast. "Take this and shoot the ropes. I'll catch him."

Nodding her understanding, she wipes the tears away from her face. "Fucking make it count, Scarlet." Handing her my pistol, there's determination in her look. I know she won't fucking fail me. Running down, narrowly hitting any of the risers, I position myself below him. "Now, Scarlet! Now!"

The crack of the gun popping off shots rings through the empty hall as pieces of the wood rain down. My brother's body falls limply into my arms, and it takes a great deal of strength to cradle him. Tearing the noose off his neck, I check for a pulse. It's awfully weak. "Call the fucking ambo! Get one here now, Scarlet."

"Got it!" she yells, running to my side. Tossing the gun to the ground, Scarlet starts to dial 911. Hearing her walk away to talk to them, I concentrate on Kyden.

"Don't you dare fucking die on me. You can't. You're my other half." I talk to him in a low tone. "I'll close up shop. Just fucking live for me." Inspecting the cuts on his arms and the etched "sins" on his chest, I tear off my cut. Stripping off my T-shirt, I tear it apart with my knife that I always carry and continue to talk to him. "Do you remember when we used to go to the park? You were always the vindictive one. If I pushed too hard, you did it slowly. If I tried to bounce you on the seesaw, you'd refuse to go back on it for weeks, knowing full well it was my favorite."

Tying the shirt strips around his arms to staunch the blood, I think of all the things I'd rather lose than him. Losing my other half would be giving up the remaining part of my soul. I have very little left of it that hasn't been tainted, but he's the reason it's there. Without him, the devils will run free. The demons that enjoy blood and retribution will be dealing it out in spades.

"Don't leave me, Ky. You keep me sane."

Hearing the ambulance screaming in the distance, getting closer and closer, I hold my brother tight. Tears that have never once left my eyes now flow in massive streams as I think of living without him. His good soul. His free spirit.

Coming back into the chapel, Scarlet tells me softly, "The ambulance should be pulling around the corner. What do you want me to tell them?"

"Tell them nothing. This is Bow business." Looking at her, I can see it. She's only ever loved him. I knew that using her to get what I wanted the other night was wrong, but I thought it would sway him. I was wrong. "Go home, Scarlet."

"But, don't—"

Stroking Kyden's hair away from his face, I say, "No. It's mine now to fix."

She walks closer. "Don't leave, Kyden. We're nothing without you. We're tortured souls without you."

She couldn't be more correct. Looking me in the eye, fearing me like she should right now, Scarlet turns and leaves out the back of the chapel, just as the front doors open.

The sound of feet traipsing harshly across the front entrance alerts me that they've entered.

"Over here!" It's not who I thought or expected to see. Both men are wearing their cuts, grinning darkly. "What are you doing here?" But I already know full well why they're here.

"Time to pay up. The Horsemen required due payment." Holding out their guns, both bastards aim at me and my brother.

With quick succession, I feel the bullets rain down, entering my chest. Stopping to holster their guns, they smile and turn away, thinking it's over. Reaching for my piece, I know the most I have are two bullets left. Aiming, I hit both square in the chest. Teetering for a second, they look surprised, shocked at the outcome before falling face-first to the floor.

As the shock starts to settle in, I know that I'm about to join my brother if the real attendants don't show soon. "Keep the gates open for me, brother. Hell has no idea what it's in for with us." Breathing weakly, worrying about keeping him alive—the better of us—I laugh at the circumstances. Looking at the two arrows lodged in the wood above, I know he needed one last strike. The second shot struck straight through the first, splitting it down the center. One arrow, two pieces. One Devil's Guide and two sons. A matched set to lose their lives in this church.

Kind of ironic.

Using the last of my strength, I say, "I love you, brother. I'll see you in death. Blessed is the arrow that strikes true."

Don't miss out!

Visit the website below and you can sign up to receive emails whenever Kerri Ann publishes a new book. There's no charge and no obligation.

https://books2read.com/r/B-A-SLJG-BSTT

BOOKS 2 READ

Connecting independent readers to independent writers.

Also by Kerri Ann

The Broken Bows
Rook
King

Watch for more at https://www.authorkerriann.com.

About the Author

Mother of two insanely (well trained) sarcastic men, wife to a dangerously smolder inducing grumble bunny (fireman), and friend to some amazing ladies (you know who you are). Thanks for reading, thanks for being a friend, and I look forward to meeting you in the future for drinks, danger and laughs.

Living in Northern Ontario, Canada, Kerri loves to read, travel and find new reasons to write you fantastic love stories. Remember, not all love is clean. Dark, light, angsty, sexually charged and twisted—that's her genre.

It's heart wrenching stories where the muse directs her. As the instrument of their lives, their stories are told through piece by piece. You can hope for the good guy to win, but it won't always happen. She can't guarantee an HEA (happily ever after) or HFN (happy for now), because life doesn't always have those.

Enjoy the OMG's and tears. Tear your hair out, toss a book or two, because I want you to feel their pain too. As they live it, you can absorb it on the pages.

Website: https://www.authorkerriann.com

Goodreads: https://www.goodreads.com/author/show/15556808.Kerri_Ann

BookBub: www.bookbub.com/authors/kerri-ann

Instagram: www.instagram.com/authorkerriann

My Website: www.authorkerriann.com

Facebook page https://www.facebook.com/LoveandDreams

Twitter https://twitter.com/Daresanddreams

MeWe https://mewe.com/i/kerri/ann

Book+Main Bites https://www.bookandmainbites.com/kerriann

Tumblr https://www.tumblr.com/follow/authorkerriann

Read more at https://www.authorkerriann.com.